*To Jacob*  J.K.

*To Jack Lilly D'Cruz*  J.M.

Text copyright © 1994 by Jenny Koralek
Illustrations copyright © 1994 by James Mayhew

All rights reserved.

First U.S. edition 1994

Library of Congress Cataloging-in-Publication Data

Koralek, Jenny.
The boy and the cloth of dreams / Jenny Koralek ; illustrated by James Mayhew.
—1st U.S. ed.
Summary: A boy who has torn holes in his cloth of dreams
experiences nightmares at his grandmother's house and must find his own
courage in order to help her mend the cloth.
ISBN 1-56402-349-4
[1. Nightmares—Fiction.   2. Fear—Fiction.   3. Courage—Fiction.
4. Grandmothers—Fiction.]   I. Mayhew, James, 1964– ill.  II. Title.
PZ7.K8363Bo    1994
[E]—dc20        93-23091

4 6 8 10 9 7 5 3

Printed in Hong Kong

The pictures in this book were done in watercolor and inks with cloth collage.

Candlewick Press
2067 Massachusetts Avenue
Cambridge, Massachusetts 02140

# The Boy
### and the
# Cloth of Dreams

JENNY KORALEK

ILLUSTRATED BY
JAMES MAYHEW

CANDLEWICK PRESS
CAMBRIDGE, MASSACHUSETTS

There was once a boy
who was getting ready to
visit his grandmother
when he tripped on his
cloth of dreams and tore it.

His grandmother had made the cloth of dreams and spread it over his cradle when he was born. "It will keep the dark night things away," she said to his mother, "but only, of course, until he is big enough to forge his own courage."

Thanks to the cloth of dreams, the boy had never yet known a bad night, but there it now lay with two large holes in it.

"Never mind," said his mother. "Give it to your grandmother and she will most surely mend it."

But when the boy got to his grandmother's house, the swing was waiting for him under the apple tree, the doves were calling to be fed, the goldfish were blowing bubbles in the lily pond, and the sundial was telling him it was suppertime.

In the kitchen the table creaked with all his favorite food—salty, spicy, sugary, and sharp, hot and cold and fizzy.

In the bedroom the pillows were punchy, the mattress was bouncy, and when he drew the cloth of dreams up to his chin, his grandmother lit a candle and told him the kind of stories he liked best, stories with rhyme and without reason.

So of course the boy forgot all about the holes in the cloth of dreams, and by the dim candlelight his grandmother did not see them. She kissed him good night and made her way to her room.

When the boy fell asleep with moonlight on his face, a chain of nightmares came out through the holes in the cloth of dreams, and as they were new to him he was quite helpless before them.

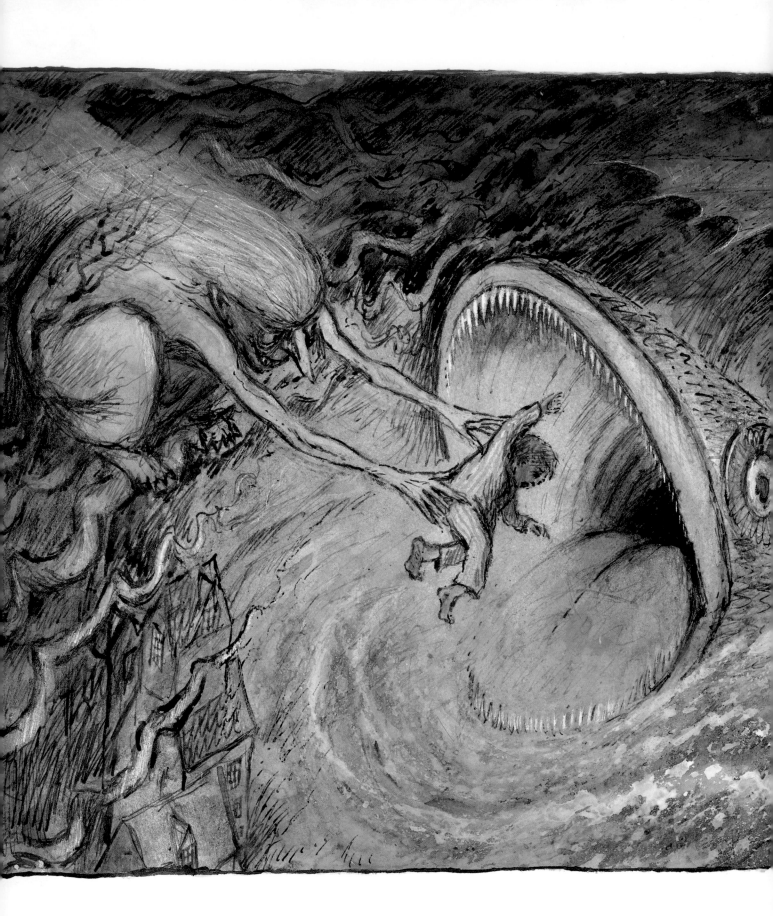

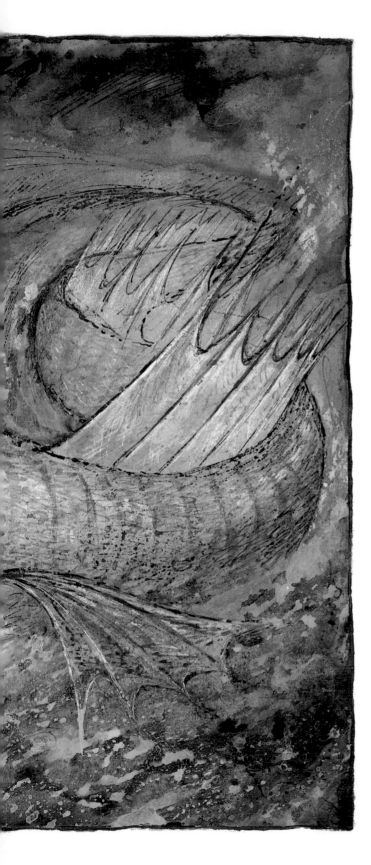

A frightful hag chased him through woods full of leafless trees with branches like claws and caught him and tickled him with long, stabbing, bony fingers, and no sooner was the boy free of her than he fell into the jaws of a huge fish.

Down he fell into its hot, steamy belly, which was so big the boy could stand up in it. He shouted and shouted for his grandmother but no sounds came out of his mouth.

When at last the fish opened its toothy jaws, the boy fell out with a crash and woke up and found he was lying on the floor shivering with the torn cloth of dreams beside him.

Then he remembered the holes and what his mother had said to him: "Give it to your grandmother and she will most surely mend it." So he picked up the cloth of dreams and opened the door of his bedroom.

But oh! how dark the landing was, how big and dark. His grandmother had taken the candle with her and the moon had disappeared behind a huge cloud. He could see a light glowing under his grandmother's door, but that only made it worse because he could make out shapes all around him, uncertain shapes that might be the things that were there in the day but might be things that came in the night.

The boy was afraid to turn back and afraid to go on. His body trembled and his teeth chattered, but he fixed his eye on the glow from his grand-mother's room and set forth with his fears across the dark, shape-filled landing.

He stubbed his toe on some strange thing and hit his elbow on another. Each step he took made a fearful creak; something sighed in the curtains, and for a moment he lost sight of the light.

And suddenly he was there in the doorway of his grand-mother's room, holding out the torn cloth of dreams.

"Horrible things came through these holes," he said, "and I made a dark crossing to come to you. Please will you mend it?"

"With your help," said his grandmother, "I most surely will."

And she picked up an empty basket and led him to a little door he had not seen before and set him on a steep stairway.

"You must fetch me threads from the sun and threads from the moon," said his grandmother.

"B–but," stammered the boy.

"No buts," said his grandmother. "I am too old to climb the stairs."

Gripped with fear, the boy climbed the stairs one by one and came out onto a flat place on the roof that seemed to be touching the sky.

The silver moon was fading into a green sky and the golden sun was rising into a rosy sky.

The boy had never before seen anything so beautiful and powerful, so quiet and so certain.

All the same he was terrified. Surely the sun would burn him. Surely the moon would freeze him.

But surely his grandmother would not let harm come to him. After all, it was she who had made the cloth of dreams to protect him.

So the boy put out a brave hand and pulled at the sun's first rays, which he found were as warm as his mother's smile. Then he pulled at the moon's last rays, which he found were as cold and as sharp as his fears in the dark, but he went on standing there firmly in his bare feet, pulling at the rays until the basket was full.

Then he bounded down the stairs and gave it to his grandmother.

In the twinkling of an eye, she threaded the gold and threaded the silver and flashed her needle through the cloth of dreams and suddenly the gaping holes had completely disappeared.

"There you are," said his
grandmother, holding out
the cloth of dreams to the boy.
"Not that you need it anymore.
Tonight you have forged your
own courage."

"Have I?" said the boy in
a whisper.

"You have," said his grandmother.

And they smiled at one
another.

Then the boy hurried back to
his room to get dressed.

As the world was stepping
out of night into a new day, he
ran downstairs two at a time,
out into the garden, across the
dewy grass, jumped onto the
swing and set it going higher
than he ever had before.